The Imperfect Garden

The Imperfect Garden

MELISSA ASSALY APRIL DELA NOCHE MILNE

Fitzhenry & Whiteside

195 Allstate Parkway, Markham, ON   L3R 4T8

Published in Canada by Fitzhenry & Whiteside

195 Allstate Parkway, Markham, ON   L3R 4T8

Published in the United States by Fitzhenry & Whiteside

311 Washington Street, Brighton, MA   02135

10 9 8 7 6 5 4 3 2 1

Fitzhenry & Whiteside acknowledges with thanks the Canada Council for the Arts and the Ontario Arts Council for their support of our publishing program. We acknowledge the financial support of the Government of Canada through the Canada Book Fund (CBF) for our publishing activities.

ONTARIO ARTS COUNCIL
CONSEIL DES ARTS DE L'ONTARIO
an Ontario government agency
un organisme du gouvernement de l'Ontario

Canada Council   **Conseil des Arts**
for the Arts   **du Canada**

Text and cover design by Kerry Designs

Printed in China by Sheck Wah Tong Printing Ltd

www.fitzhenry.ca

Library and Archives Canada Cataloguing in Publication

Assaly, Melissa, author

Imperfect garden / Melissa Assaly ;

illustrations by April Dela Noche Milne.

ISBN 978-1-55455-408-9 (hardcover).

I. Milne, April Dela Noche, illustrator II. Title.

PS8601.S675I47 2019   jC813'.   C2018-904761-5

Publisher Cataloging-in-Publication Data (U.S.)

Names: Assaly, Melissa, author. |

Dela Noche Milne, April, illustrator.

Title: The Imperfect Garden / Melissa Assaly ;

April Dela Noche Milne.

Description: Markham, Ontario :

Fitzhenry & Whiteside, 2019. | Summary: "A mother and child garden their family vegetable patch for food and health through the seasons and come to appreciate home-made produce – with tips for family gardening and green living" – Provided by publisher.

Identifiers: ISBN 978-1-55455-408-9 (hardcover)

Subjects: LCSH: Gardening -- Juvenile fiction. | Natural foods -- Juvenile fiction. | Cooking (Natural foods) – Juvenile fiction. | BISAC: JUVENILE FICTION / Health & Daily Living / General. | JUVENILE FICTION / Nature & the Natural World / General.

Classification: LCC PZ7.1A873Im |DDC [E] – dc23

To Jay, for being a constant ray of sunshine in my life.
— Melissa

With love for my nanay, who so loved to garden, and papa, who loves good food.
—April

My mom and I like to grow some of our own food. We plant a garden each Spring in our backyard. I help water the soil.

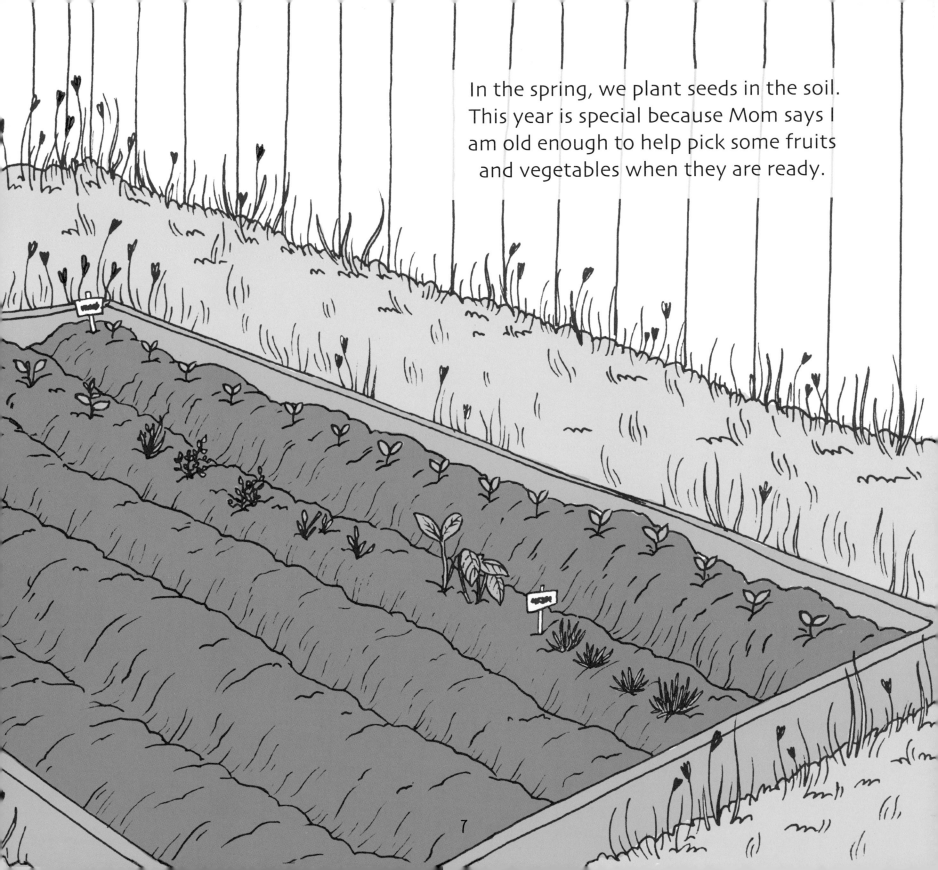

In the spring, we plant seeds in the soil. This year is special because Mom says I am old enough to help pick some fruits and vegetables when they are ready.

7

In June, we find cucumbers growing on vines in all kinds of twirly-whirly shapes! Mom finds one that looks like the letter J, the first letter in my name, Jay. I find one that looks like a boomerang but I probably shouldn't throw it.

"Why are the cucumbers at the supermarket all straight?", I ask Mom. "They throw the twirly-whirly ones in the garbage because shoppers like to buy straight ones," she says. I think the twirly-whirly cucumbers are amazing!

9

In July, Mom says the carrots are ready to pick. How can she tell? Carrots grow deep in the ground. Mom shows me how to grab the green, leafy carrot tops and pull them up carefully.

Hmm… This carrot looks like it has two legs. Mom says carrots come in all shapes and sizes. We are just used to the ones in the store.

11

After we pull a few more carrots,
I wash them and Mom peels them. I take
a bite of my two-legged carrot and a
bite of the ordinary-looking carrot.
They are both crunchy and delicious.

In August, it is time to pick apples. We need a ladder to reach them. I pick enough to fill my basket. We are going to bake apple pies!

Some of our apples are red, and some are red and yellow. Some are smooth and shiny, and some are bumpy. I find one that looks like a funny face! Mom laughs when I try to make the same funny face.

Mom says all apples taste delicious in pies. We peel them and cut them up and bake two "Mom and Jay" pies. We save one for us and give one to Mr. Jackson next door.

19

I am glad we had enough apples to make two "Mom and Jay" pies. If we had thrown away the bumpy apples we would have only had enough for one pie.

I like eating food that comes from our backyard. Mom says I am helpful and have a green thumb. I think all my fingers look the same, but she says having a green thumb means I am a really good gardener.

22

In October, the days get colder and shorter, and we have eaten all the food from our garden. It is time to go to the grocery store to buy the fruits and vegetables we need.

24

The food here seems so ordinary. Where are the two-legged carrots, the twirly-whirly cucumbers, and the funny-faced apples? Don't grownups know they all taste the same? Even better, maybe?

I ask the grocer, "Don't you have any twirly-whirly, lumpy, bumpy fruits and vegetables?"

30

My eyes light up when I find the three-legged carrots, a cucumber shaped like the number six, and more. And they cost less money than the boring ones!

There are kiwis shaped like hearts,
potatoes with lumps,
and the silliest red
peppers ever. And I can't
wait to eat them!

SALE

30% SALE

SALE

50%

REDUCED
FRUITS and
VEGETABLES

33

Author's Note

Reducing our food waste is one of the best ways to care for our environment. It is estimated that 168 million tonnes of food are wasted in North America each year. Many items are thrown out simply for looking imperfect. At the same time it is estimated that 12.7% of Canadians don't know where their next meal is coming from.

The future of our earth depends on humans taking better care of it than they have in the past. Even small actions, like the ones in this book, can add up to big changes if many people take part.

Tips for Planting With children

Gardening engages children in the act of growing and informs them about where food comes from. Planting with children can be done in the garden, on a balcony, or in the classroom.

To grow your own plants, all you need are seeds, soil, water, and sunlight. I highly recommend starting with vegetables that are easy to grow. I've had great success with green peas, yellow beans, pumpkin, and cucumber plants. You don't need a garden. Large containers work for smaller spaces like balconies or small yards. Clear containers let you see the roots of the plants as they grow.

Teach children how to water plants just enough to moisten the soil (excessive amounts of water will drown your plants). One tip is to use a spray bottle instead of a watering can to help control the flow of water to the soil. Children can also help with weeding and picking the fruit and vegetables when they are ready to harvest. Everyone enjoys eating foods they have helped to grow themselves. And remember...your fruits and veggies might look a little different but they will taste just as good. Maybe better!

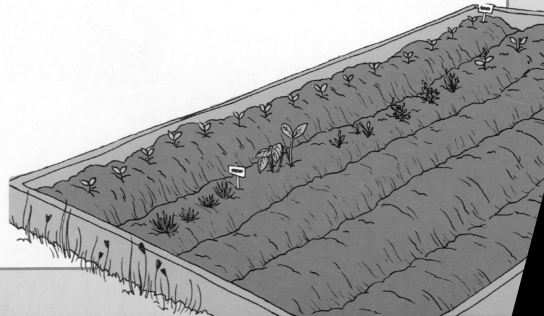